Larry Skadarry
The Forgetful Tooth Fairy

Written by Whitney Beatty
Illustrated by Becca Kaiser

To Kelly, who gave me the idea.
To Ed, who gave me the name.
And to Lucy, who gave me grief about not
dedicating my first book to her.

- WB

Above the clouds, but below the stars,
(if you reach the moon, you've gone too far)

There's a magical world that sparkles with white,
from canines and molars that shine clean and bright.

It's Tooth Fairy Kingdom, built all out of teeth!
They buy them of course - no one here is a thief.

When a little kid's tooth comes loose with a wiggle,
one Tooth Fairy's list gets a magic new squiggle.

LOST TEETH
Magnus Bryan
Graham Matthew
Delaney Emma
Jack Attack
Lucy Willamina

The name and address tells them just where to be,
to buy a fresh tooth for a nominal fee.*

*The exact amount varies, it's based on inflation and COLA and other accounting equations.

They scoop up the teeth then fly back to their home,
to build bridges, tall towers, a new concert dome!

But one fairy's projects are never quite done.
His list grows and grows after each nightly run.

On the outskirts of town, in a house bright and airy,
lives a forgetful tooth fairy named Larry Skadarry.

Larry loves to collect each tooth that's extracted,
but Larry Skadarry is quickly distracted.

Every night he sets out, armed with his list,
sure he'll get to each home, but there's always a twist.

One night, shooting stars caught
his gaze for three hours.

Another he spent counting petals on flowers.

Once he met a lost owl who he helped find her nest.
She insisted he stay for a meal as her guest.

On his way to a house where the sea meets the land,
he whiled away hours making castles of sand.

Next night he lost focus while flying to Earth,
and landed in Paris instead of in Perth.

Seamus
Fiona
Nora
Will
Brooke
Avery
Grant
Alex
Piper
Reese
Shay
Kaden
Logan
XS

Vi

Henr

Colin

harlotte

Eli

LOST
TEETH

Tommy

Joey

Lily

Mason

Liam

Claire

Cate

Each time he's off track in his comings and goings,
more kids lose their teeth and his list keeps on growing!

So if your tooth is still there when you wake for the day,
know that Larry Skadarry is still on his way.

And one night very soon he'll come pick up your tooth...

...so that maybe - one day - he can finish his roof.